Rated

R

The Poetic Reminisces
of a Recalcitrant and
Unrepentant
Roue

E.S. Cuny

Published by
Legacy Literary Publishing
First Edition

Legacy Literary Publishing
PO Box 220
Davilla TX 76523
Phone 254-654-7205

Edited by Tony Burnett
ISBN:978-1-952224-99-7

Rated

R

*The Poetic Reminisces
of a Recalcitrant and
Unrepentant
Roue*

E.S. Cuny

Table of Contents

3 Covering the Course — 1

Plush Knee — 2

Comet-ery on the Pattern of Life — 3

The Beauty of Women — 4

Thorough Curvature — 5

L' Dolce Vita — 6

Four Dresses — 7

Dandelions — 9

Love's Shadows — 11

High Tea — 11

Barriers — 12

Outside the Laundromat — 13

At the Mermaid Bar and Grill — 14

She Sleeps Now — 15

The Time of Sighs — 16

Tomato Picking — 17

3 Things You Must Do — 19

The Address For All Times Sake — 20

Pussy Willows — 21

*To the lovers left,
or lost — but not forgotten —
and thank God for them!*

3 Covering the Course

Love is, what makes an
ordinary day, special.
That's it, in a nutshell.

> When I clean the teapot
> the spout leaves a wet spot
> reminds my little darlin'
> smiling in her bed.

Wrapped in the celestial song
nothing we did here
can be counted as wrong.

Plush Knee

I think that I shall never see
a thing so sexy as her knee,
slinking down beneath her skirt
　　　－ she is such a flirt.

As the party 'round us swirls
she gives me a glance through her curls,
at the doorway gives a finger's quirk,
　　　she is *such* a flirt!

In the darkness she takes my hand
together we find a grassy strand
where we tease each other 'til it hurts,
　　　Yes! She's quite the flirt!

And as she lays back on the ground
and spreads her thighs, so soft and round
then beckons me join her in the dirt,
　　　Oh, *she is such a flirt!*

As her legs wrap round my behind
and we do the 'bump and grind';
Thus fulfilling the purpose in life
　　　of life's little flirt.

Comet-ery on the Pattern of Life

On learning of the role frozen comets played
in bringing the water now covering the Earth,
I stand again astounded and amazed
at Life's ability to germinate the barren and inert.

As hordes of meteors gravitated onto the planet,
their contrails crisscrossing the atmosphere,
until they struck the continental granite
piercing their payloads deep into the multi-cratered sphere.

Eventually, we're told, waters rose unconstrained
while comets kept coming and plowing through,
splashing into seas that melted away what the ice contained:
the amino elixirs that form me and you.

Amazing not only the actions, but also the form established
in the way water quenched our planetary thirst,
by absorbing the millions of comets the eons could brandish,
then release from their inner cores, the core of the universe.

This is the only pattern life found it could invoke,
a pathway to prosper on seemingly insensate substrates,
eternally repeating in form, from acorns falling into oaks,
and even into the microscopic realms of us vertebrates.

The Beauty of Women

It's the beauty in women that's seen when they're
looking at this or that, and when they're pointing out
this or that, when they're moving this way or that,
when they're talking on cell phones about this
or that, or when walking toward or waving back,
hands fluttering or quickly covering … perhaps a smile?

Yet their beauty is not just in their physical image
but in their way of sustaining healthy relationships,
which are the underpinnings of a thriving society.
For all the wistfulness in observation as they weave together
their threads of conversation, realization dawns that they
are the foundation and keepers – and hope – of civilization.

Admiring only the bits and parts will take its toll,
when the truth of beauty encompasses the whole.

Thorough Curvature

I watched her slip past
through the curvature of glass
her long train streaming out behind her.

Just 'a tall sip of water' without urgency,
her garment revealing every tendency
as she slipped past.

"Just a sip?" was all she asked,
and sipped from my glass
as her long train spun out around her.

Lips slipped on the rim,
met mine in a silent sin
and she slipped on past.

I set down the glass
as she looked over and back
at the train streaming out behind her.

I realize with a gasp
at long last the die is cast:
eyes filled with music and maze,
I join the train of men strung out behind her.

L' Dolce Vita

(Some think)
it was just a bistro,
the Dolce Vita, but
like its name it was much
more. In fact, it was where
the arbiters of values in this world met.

(They were)
young women
who sat at tables,
who set the lines
amid
the talk of girls.
That is, as long as
they didn't know
they were.

(But)
once realized, they aged out,
and that power forfeit.
Not unlike the
Dolce Vita
itself.

Four Dresses

I.

There are four dresses that stand out
in the many a woman will wear in life.
These dresses mark major stages of passage
that a woman will desire and bear. They are:
The Prom Dress, the Bridesmaid's Couture,
the Wedding Gown, and the Widow's Veils.
In a way, they're all a gift wrapping,
a present from the current state to the future,
        and the past.

II.

The Prom Dress's elegance says:
I am coming, and, *I am leaving,*
all at the same time. The Prom is
one statement to the other girls
and a different one to the other side.
At the Prom, the guys see the beauty
but don't realize the meaning, too busy
tugging at their collars or spiking the punch.
But the girls size it all up. They know
the signals, and the outside
        beckons.

III.

The Wedding Whites say: *Here's what
you're getting,* and *Here I go,* then it's off
on a run. The Gown is a giving of one to one,
a life hoisted up in a phrase, *I do.*
At the wedding there's too much event
to appreciate its style, its accessories and train,
as it flows down the aisle. All we see is a radiant smile.
By the time we can get around to enjoying
the garment's finer points, it's gone,
removed for the reception, protected from
the spillage and sweat yet to come, packed away,
        out of sight, saved.

IV.

In the end the Widow's Black says, *There you go.*
and *Here's all that's left,* allowing her in stillness
to think, *I am coming home to abide,* waiting
to decide where to pick up after a life let off.
The dress and veils are both the Widow's grieving
the loss, and a light of hope for
        the life ahead.

V.

But my favorite is the Bridesmaid's Couture,
the dress in-between them all.
The Bridesmaid's colors say: *Here I am!*
I am ready! and each stands alone in a group.
Past the yearning for independence,
and before the plighting of the merger,
with just a hint of the widows' weeds
in the clock on the back wall of the hall.
The Bridesmaid's dress says — *Unwrap me!*
As the other's do in their own way, but not
with the same panache of the unstated:
        Now.

VI.

The dress rises from the floor, in purple
or yellows or blues, with sparkles or stripes
or perhaps dappled with contrasting hues.
It follows the curve of the leg and hugs
the derriere, angles around the hips,
then sliding over ribs, upwardly lifting
the eye to the flowing fit befitting the breasts
in magnificent expostulation. Then the arms
and neck rise from the dress, as flowers
from a vase. Yet this bouquet holds a precision
of passion held in check, to be subtly
cocked towards those found most alluring,
in desirous decision for a readied incursion.
The Bridesmaid's dress and bearing is a call
to those she has in her sights: *Unwrap. Me.*
        Now!

Dandelions

Waiters file in as the gathering ends,
past brooms pushing down halls nightly,
          and dandelions return to flight.

The celebration is finished, leftovers left over.
A loosened-tie partier deals himself from a deck missing cards,
a porter with trays picks up crumpled napkins
and empty glasses, winds around a pair
of dancers standing still to fading chords.
The couples who came together and
the pairs who met have already left,
with giggles or farewells to friends, letting in
the surf sounds of passing cars swooshing by
          as exit doors opened.

In groups of threes and fours a last
coterie of ladies, a passel of men
cluster and linger by the door saying goodbye.
Hoping to but not having made a match
they leave as halves leaving the comradery
of cordial drinks and wandering eyes;
of unfinished conversations finished
with a nod; a dismissive wave, or even a belch.
Some share a parting word with the last few
who enjoyed the warmth of the stereo.
Once outside, a quick huddle with final friends,
reassuring glances of grimaces and grins,
some wistfully glancing over shoulders,
yearning for the other half they won't
be helping home. A last borrowing of cigarettes,
          a passing flame.

Inside that hall, walls palpable, carpet touchable
plates clatter, telephones buzz, the last one remaining
flips over a one-eyed jack, puts down the deck
grunts to no one in particular, shrugs on a coat and
with random thoughts in a hazy head heads out the door
like the burned-out character at the end of a novel,
to walk down darkened streets as they receive
          a nightly washing.

Janitors lock up after the party dies,
brooms push down darkened halls,
          and dandelion return to flight.

Love's Shadows

Lines crease across my forehead and arc
as if gulls on wing, circling over water
in a graceful lie to the turbulence beneath.
Late into the night I stare out windows
while sight wanders as aimlessly as thoughts
sifting through shadows, with darkness fading
           in and out of memory.

Along the window sill plants are set, their leaves
tuned to the stars gathering in what light they may,
the way I screen the darkness for you. And carelessly
my thoughts have returned to you again.
It is false hope to imagine you are out there
rustling shadows.   I do not expect to see your face
etched in the glass pane. No, what I know of you
           is movement.

A turn in your walk as you approached, a smile
caressed your lips as the track of some high-soaring
peregrine on wing and our souls flickered in greeting.
I hear a noise – the shadows might contain you?
Again, my thoughts take flight over murky waters
           and fly to you.

I still can't believe your last movement was to turn,
turn and walk away. From all the time we had
that made us glad to have found each other, leaving me
to wonder deep into every everlasting night,
           will you come back?

High Tea

Smokey fragrance pierced
by blue eyes, in every sip now
of Lapsang Su Chow..

Barriers

But a single aisle separates our tables
keeping us across from each other.
Otherwise in this crowed diner
we'd be sharing one. This way
we're close without being
close, a mutual
deceiving.

Yet
I can glance
without being obvious
at the rings in her nose, the tats
on her toes and arms and neck and the rising
and heaving of her shoulders and breasts
with the intermittent sighing
of her breath as she eyes
some digital reads
from her
device.

No way
to approach,
scoot a bit closer
gently interrupt with
a smile or a reach across to ask
a question without being obvious
while she's still lost, oblivious to all
except tablet and cell, an invisible barrier that
remains erect between us leaving, nothing to tell.

Outside the Laundromat

Early Houston morning
in a run-down part of town
vacant streets and sidewalks
         not a soul around.

Except a weathered lady
across the street who languidly leans,
against the wall in go-go boots,
a halter top and cut-off
         denim jeans.

She lights another cigarette
while waiting to be seen
oblivious to the sign overhead
touting the laundromat's machines:
         "Speed Queen".

The store fronts are all empty
not a person or a sound,
only a distant church bell's ring
         as I turn the car around.

At the Mermaid Bar and Grill

She met me at her table
Neon red and blue pulsating outside
she was spinning her shell,

a pendant dangling luxuriously
held within a breasty gasp: Nothing is true.
She met me at her table.

Though being and description
are but a net of words, she played life the way
she was spinning her shell.

Precarious the tongue that does not behold
the windy words of meaning, such as:
she met me at her table.

But atop a winding staircase
deep green shadows led beyond velvet red curtains
where she was spinning her shell.

Consider not the coral briny
nor the mother of pearl there inlaid, merely
she met me at the table
where she was spinning her shell.

She Sleeps Now

She pulls on the sheets
as she rolls to her side,
over the curve of her hips
they gently glide…
Ah, what would I give
to see her at dawn?
Perhaps with a smile,
or a blurry yawn
her body stretching out
with arms open to my own.

Should I awake to confess
these mixed up feelings?
No, she had a hard day
and we had our turn, now
it's time for her sleeping.

With a kiss on her neck,
a whisper in her ear
a little sigh of longing,
a pat on her rear,
I key out her door, then
pause, caught in revere.

But domesticity calls
and as I depart
wishes turn to ashes
in flames of my heart.

The Time of Sighs

When the white hot heat
which is squeezed from deep
red blood, passes in passionless
embrace, when blue stones set in silver
no longer clatter and jingle in joyous removal
along the moonlit trace but lie, listless, next
to the bed; then is the sign of the sigh
certain, and with the dawning of
recognition comes the drawing
of lines, the drawing
of curtains.
For
a sigh
once given
to express nothing,
next is received in return.
Finally it's known that it's drawn
not in the manner of a dagger in anger
but more as an exit of breath at the severance
of ties and the slipping of bonds, a mutual
acknowledgment that sand has slipped
through the hourglass, and
l'petit affaire d'couer
has run its course.

Tomato Picking

On a country road by a farmer's road-side plot
I pulled over in a moment of inspiration,
mesmerized by a tomato plant
that had caught my fascination.
It was a magnificent bush, full and vibrant
swaying just outside the farm's scrutiny.
Something behind a jostling movement
had quite piqued my curiosity.

Leafy skirts lifted in a lilting breeze
coyly eyeing me eyeing the offered sight.
I reached out and gave a gentle squeeze,
held the round firmness plump and ripe.
Falling to the ground I followed down,
spreading petals wide, I partook in delight.

Now, most tomatoes you get these days
are set out green, cold, almost nonchalant.
Little more than a salad's prelude
to the main entree in a restaurant.
Or they're whipped up to a frenzy
then are lost with others in some mix.
Or even dressed up to be a bit saucy
as in a hot salsa, served with chips.

But this was different. Out in the sun,
warm and young, with the promises
of a taste that was heavenly.
I was guided down, down, down
deep into a viscousness
of a passion consumed quite languidly.
And afterward, the taste on lips
will be worn in memory with epaulets …

… and well past the farmer's gesticulations
and angry curses and mad accusations
when finding his favorite flower
warmly fecund in the little bower,
on the field's edge where he'd wandered:
plucked, yes – but not squandered!
Dodging vicious hurled curses and epithets
 – and even a blast of shotgun pellets –
I ran to my car and got rolling!
But to my regret, I have never had yet,
a tastier tomato than that which was stolen.

3 Things You Must Do

You must have dinner at *El Reina's* restaurant
where they don't bother asking you what you want.
And you must attend *Hatrtigan's Cinema Screen*
where they never show the last reel of the final scene.

Oh, you must have a drunken conversation with Bill English
and Sallie Stranger, with John Hardin and Marilyn on the list,
so many things intensely discussed and understood –
in the morning all you remember is the light on wood.

And make the time under an astrodome's cover
to spend the night with a jigsaw lover.

The Address For All Times Sake

I. Revolving

I know you're a woman
who still has hangups
issues, whatever, about it ...
but I still

       want

          with you

to make mad

             passionate

                 love.

II. Reminisce-sense

Oh, I remember, though not why it was not to be,
but that she gave of herself so willingly.
How dappled moonlight played on rounded breasts
shimmering and taut ... But the time was not right
for us to keep our hold beyond the night.
I wasn't ready nor could have settled,
if I was a jerk I hope she's forgiven,
but I'll never forget, and I'll keep hope,
she's with someone somewhere more deserving.

III. Reverie

So I raise a glass: to the lovers left behind,
and whatever it is that brings them to mind.
Here's to the tits or pricks or smiles or wits –
whatever reminds you of whatever you miss,
wistfully maybe, longingly hopefully,
for both the ladies and the gents that's
causing your pausing and wondering
      "what if"...

So stop a minute stranger,
here's to the memories of lovers lost,
and here's to the ones gave us the toss!
Lift a glass or wink an eye, thank them
      and good-bye!

Pussy Willows

Pussy willow, pussy willow
          so white, so dark
so soft, so sharp
          when broken off.
Where are you now
          my little pussy willow?

For those of you who may be disappointed
upon meeting this old grandfather from Austin
please remember these are *Reminisces* after all!

These are a looking back at times that were enjoyed,
or witnessed, or maybe overheard or wished, or even …
All-in-all these hopefully provide some enjoyment
of our mutual human condition.

Thanks and a tip of the hat goes to the great poet,
Yuri Yevtushenko for insight into of the true cost of certain pilfered
goods. And a grateful nod to the hard work and patience of
Tony Burnett.

Please note, some poems included here are part of other pieces
but but stand quite well on their own.
Always open for comments at: ifandorx9@gmail.com
And don't forget
the *3 Things You Must Do* –
have at it!